Florence I. Duncan

Ye Last Sweet Thing in Corners

Being ye faithful drama of ye artists' vendetta

Florence I. Duncan

Ye Last Sweet Thing in Corners
Being ye faithful drama of ye artists' vendetta

ISBN/EAN: 9783337343736

Printed in Europe, USA, Canada, Australia, Japan

Cover: Foto ©Andreas Hilbeck / pixelio.de

More available books at **www.hansebooks.com**

Ye Last Sweet Thing in Corners

Being

Ye Faithful Drama

Ye Artists' Vendetta

Duncan & Hall,
Publishers.
Philadelphia.

EPISTLE DEDICATORY.

My Dear Lord Dufferin :

May I dedicate this little play to you in remembrance of the many happy hours at Rideau bearing especially in mind all that is associated with that never-to-be-forgotten night when your Epilogue was spoken—

> " *And oft at home when Christmas fire-logs burn*
> *Our pensive thoughts instinctively will turn*
> *To this fair city with her crown of towers,*
> *And all the joys and friends that once were ours,*
> *And oft shall yearning fancy fondly fill*
> *This hall with guests, and conjure up at will*
> *Each dear familiar face, each kindly word—*"

Faithfully,
THE AUTHOR.

Philadelphia, Christmas, 1880.

TIME—To-day. PLACE—A Conundrum.

ACT I.
THE PLOT—*In a Studio.*

ACT II.
HIGH ART—*In a Barn.*

ACT III.
HOME—*In a Cottage.*

DRAMATIS PERSONÆ.

RAPHAEL GAMBOGE.................A Painter.

IL BACIO MODDLE.................A Sculptor.

BAROUCHE BROWN.... ....An Art Critic.

DR. SAM FLOYD...........An Unemotional Physician.

NATHANIEL BOBBIN ....An Enthusiast in Soap.

ALFRESCO DADO.............⎫

MAUD CASHMERE BOUQUET.......⎬ Daughters to Brown.

CONSUELA RENAISSANCE.........⎭

MISS ALHAMBRA FRIEZE ....Their High-Church Friend.

MISS CAIRNGORM ....A Woman Reporter.

ANGELICO BEN. CEL. BAXTER...Colored page to the Browns.

COSETTES' ANKLES.. (Cosette being Brown's meek handmaiden.)

BILL BYLES...........An Angel in the oyster business.

CRICKET.................A bit of egg shell china.

GRASSHOPPER ....An Egyptian Mummy.

STUMPS...................An Old Greek Marble.

POLICEMEN, CONNOISSEURS, ETC.

ACT I. THE PLOT.

Scene I.— *The Studio.*

Enter RAPHAEL GAMBOGE, *excitedly holding a newspaper in his hand.*

Gamboge. I don't mind the fellow making an infernal fool of himself as long as some other idiot can be found to pay him twenty dollars a column for it, but I wish to heaven he would make an ass of himself on some other subject than Art! Was ever such a lot of rubbish palmed off on an unsuspecting public! [*Reads.*] "There is an indefinable something which steals upon the beholder, a lack of symphonic treatment, so to speak—a subtle idea—er—er—that is to say—aw—he—in fact he does not grasp his subject boldly, and there is a lack of a sense of vacancy about his sky, as it were, that seems to express, clumsy handling—Ah-h-h! The Old Masters! They were the glorious fellows." D—n the Old Masters! If I had this ill-conditioned mule in the open air, I'd let him know pretty precious quick if I could not handle a subject boldly and give him such a sense of vacancy, regarding the sky, as would send him home on a shutter!

Enter MODDLE.

Moddle. Halloo, Gam, how *is* things? Somehow you don't look happy! Oh, ah, you've been reading the Fog Whistle, have you? I thought you had sworn off on reading criticisms! I would smile at such rot—smile philosophically, Gam.

Gamboge. Teach me your philosophic smile, will you? So you have seen his notice of your Jephtha's daughter?"

Moddle. No! where? what does he say?

[*Takes the paper from* GAMBOGE *and reads.*]

Moddle [*in a rage*]. Why hang this idiotic drivel! He has mixed me up with another man. [*Slaps the paper furiously.*] Here he says my Jephtha's daughter looks like a pickle-eating graduate of the public school, a cadaverous female that ought with my Bacchus to make a pair—(my Bacchus!) exhibited last year at the Academy, which had the appearance of being modeled from Pork and after re-named Jack Spratt and wife, the Society for the prevention of Cruelty to Animals should demand that both be ground to powder for the culture of cabbage—why the d— fool Chizzle did Bacchus. Now Gam, what the devil are you making that face for?

Gamboge. I was not aware that I was making a face. I was watching for the first beam of your philosophic smile.

Moddle. H'm, well you must admit that compared with myself he has let you down easy. But I swear—by all the Chizzles and chisels—animate and inanimate, I'll be even with Brown before snow is on the ground.

Gamboge [*seizing his hand*]. And I'll help you.

[*A knock is heard.*]

Moddle. There's some one, I'll be o–p–h—see you later.

[*Exit* MODDLE, *side door.*

[GAMBOGE, *after a hasty glance about the apartment, opens door.*]

Enter fat, over-dressed OLD LADY, *with over-dressed* YOUNG DAUGHTER, *who walk in and stare about them.*

Gamboge. How can I serve you, ladies?

Fat Old Lady. Can you finish my daughter in water and ile?

Gamboge. You wish her portrait painted, I presume, madam?

F. O. L. Lor' bless you no, we got three of 'em now. You know my man's in the provision business, and we got a painter to paint her likeness an' take it out in trade; she has just left school an' we want her to be finished in water an' ile, an' be taught to criticise the paintings in the picter galleries. My man—he was dead sot on having the other painter feller learn her and take it out in trade, but Mirandy read in the paper that he didn't put the best French paint in his pictures an' I says to Dan, says I, "Dan'l you can jest as well afford to have your daughter finished in water an' ile as them Napthas. Bacon is as good as petroleum any day." I had him there, an' he gave me a check, an' I want you to make an A 1 artist of Miranda and do it reasonable.

Miranda [*who has been staring out of the window upon the street*]. Oh Mar, there's the Napthas' carriage across the way and Eveleen has gone up stairs with her drawing book. [*Turns to Artist*] Why I thought *you* gave Miss Naptha painting lessons.

Gamboge. No, madame, I have no pupil by that name.

Miranda [*folding her wrap around her*]. O dear me, mar, we've made a mistake, I want to take lessons of the same teacher Eveleen Naptha does.

F. O. L. Laws–a–me—that's too bad ; we've got in the wrong place and raised your hopes, young man. Hope we haven't taken up your time. Mirandy, lift your dress goin' down them dirty stairs. [*Exit.*

Gamboge [*throwing himself in a chair despondently*]. The same old story ! People think no more of an artist's time ! [*A knock at the door.*] There it goes again ; another infernal bore I'll bet my dinner—if I have money enough left to get it.

[*Opens the door.*]

Enter the MISSES ALFRESCO *and* MAUD BROWN, *accompanied by a* SLENDER YOUNG MAN *sucking the end of his cane.*

Alfresco. How do you do, Mr. Gamboge? Pray don't let us disturb you—commune with your muse—just as if we were not here, we have only come to stay an hour or so and look at the pretty things.

Gamboge. I am honored, Miss Brown.

[ALFRESCO *stands in a rapture before a landscape, meanwhile* SLENDER YOUNG MAN *and* MAUD *walk about the studio criticising audibly.*]

Alfresco. How sweetly pretty. Isn't it a love! I think Papa was severe on you in the paper this morning, but he means it for your good—we must not murmur at immolation on the shrine of

Art. But really, this is lovely. It makes me think of one of Prang's happiest bits—I think after the old masters, Papa dotes on Prang; you paint in sympathy with Prang, don't you think so? I am not trying to flatter you, I assure you. Those cows are *elegant*, and the tin pail in the milkmaid's hand is *so* true to nature! And Maud, just look! What a pre-Raphaelite effect that spot of ver-digris on the pail handle has!

Gamboge. If your father is severe, you are certainly too kind.

Alfresco. What a clever fellow that Hors Concours is! And such a hard-working person, I see his paintings in almost every gallery I visit. I dare say he and you are fast friends.

Gamboge [*demurely*]. Oh yes, *Hors Concours* is a very dis-tinguished man.

Maud. Don't you think, Mr. Gamboge, that the animals in your paintings are nearly all out of drawing?

Gamboge [*biting his lip*]. I beg your pardon?

[S. Y. M. *has opened a private sketch book of studies from the nude—he and Miss* ALFRESCO *start back shocked.*]

Alfresco. Oh dear! [*Faintly.*]

Maud. What is the matter, sister mine?

Alfresco. A sudden faintness, that is all—do not mind me, I shall be better presently.

S. Y. M. [*putting up his glass at Gamboge*]. Mr. Gamboge, I am surprised at you.

Gamboge [*angrily*]. Well, my dear sir, that is a private portfolio, not intended for visitors' inspection; those studies from the nude—

S. Y. M. [*coughing*]. *Ahem!* This conversation is getting to too fine a point, remember, sir, there are ladies present.

Maud [*whispering*]. Why is it that artists are so immoral in their tendencies? See! [*Clutching* S. Y. M.'s *arm.*] He has got some woman in that room. [*Points to lay figure.*] The horrid creature!

[*Exit* MISSES BROWN *looking reproachfully and indignantly at* GAMBOGE, *followed by* S. Y. M., *who places a tract on the artist's easel.*]

Gamboge [*dejectedly*]. Another hour of this would drive me mad. What a lovely girl that Miss Brown is to look at. What a pity she is such a fool. I'll get my dinner and take the taste of this out of my mouth. [*Feels in his pockets for money.*] Eighteen, nineteen; and here's a five cent piece, twenty-four. I must have another nickle somewhere—yes—no—it's a button off my light coat—Ah, Eureka—ten cents. By Jove, here's fortune; thirty-four cents. Now for dinner a la carte. I can get beefsteak and two vegetables for twenty-five cents and one beer five cents and have four cents left for two stamps to post Mrs. DeMontague's, and Thorn's bills—or I could get veal pot pie for twenty cents and get two beers—I'm *tired* of veal, I'll get mutton stew for fifteen cents—No I won't; the amount of mutton I've consumed since the exchequer has been low is simply horrible to contemplate. I shall be going around on four legs—and hire myself out as a

model to Verbœckhoven. We'll have a fresh menu. I might get
soup, ten cents ; corned-beef hash, ten cents ; sweet potatoes, five
cents, and one beer—that's the ticket ! but hold, hold my heart,
where's my supper to come from ? I might drop in Vandyck's about
that time—no, that won't do, I was there three days ago, and it's too
thin—or to speak less vulgarly, it's not sufficiently opaque and it's
hardly a week since I took a meal at his expense. Now I'll begin
all over again. Beef's a necessity—greens a luxury, so I'll say
beef stew, fifteen cents (*they give bread with it*), and one beer—
twenty cents, ten cents left for supper and four cents for postage
stamps—I trust to Providence for breakfast, don't give up the ship
old fellow ! Commune with your muse ; and *dine* on Art ; [*makes
a face*] I felt like telling Miss Brown that my muse is a coy damsel,
that comes only to me after the studio rent is paid, that my inspir-
ation is helped by a good dinner. Dine on Art—What rot ! [*A
knock is heard*] Oh—the deuce—who is that ? [*Opens the door.*]

Enter a MOTHERLY PERSON, *a* YOUNG BRIDE, *an* ÆSTHETIC
MAIDEN, *a* WOMAN REPORTER, BROWN *of the Fog Whistle and
a* CHILD *of ten years. They smile at and nod to* GAMBOGE *or
ignore him, and walk about the room looking at the paintings.*

Motherly Person. And so you're a painter, why where's your
parents?

Gamboge. They are dead, madame.

Moth. Per. Oh, I understand. How much can you make a
week at this business ?

Gamboge. Well, really, madame, I—the fact is I can't say—

Our remuneration is greater than in some professions, but it is often precarious—

Young Bride. Mr. Gamboge—I don't see anything I like here. Can't you tell me where I can get a really *good* painting about ten by fifteen inches, to fit in a space on my wall?

Gamboge. You had better go to a dealer, madame, I don't paint for the trade.

Child. Mr. Gamboge, the face of the girl in the hammock needs a little cadmium yellow, and I don't think the drapery of her polonaise is true to nature.

[*Gamboge stares at* CHILD *and looks about to whistle or to swear.*]

Woman Reporter [*walking over to Gamboge, sotto voce*]. I'll stay till these people go, because I want you to give me some items for my Art article.

Moth. Per. Have you got a good boarding-house, young man?

Gamboge. I—I—don't board exactly—that is I—[*breaks down*].

Moth. Per. [*staring at the sofa*]. Do you sleep here all night, or how?

Brown [*the critic*]. I say Gamboge, this isn't a bad thing; is it a water color or a chromo?

Gamboge. It is—

Æsthetic Maiden [*sweetly*]. Mr. Gamboge, won't you tell me some pretty little anecdote about the Old Masters, if you are not too busy now, I want to put it in my diary.

Moth. Per. What do you have to pay for your dinner, generally speaking?

Gamboge [*Generally speaking this week I haven't had any dinner to speak about.*] That depends on my appetite, madame.

Young Bride. Mr. Gamboge, couldn't you give me a card to
some dealer who would let me have a picture cheaper on account
of my knowing you?

Gamboge. I fear it would not do any good, madame.

Moth. Per. Do you generally have a good appetite, or does the
smell of your pictures sicken you of your food?

Gamboge. Yes, sometimes I have no appetite for my dinner—
[*Aside, And sometimes I have no dinner for my appetite.*]

Child. Mr. Gamboge, didn't you make that pedestal out of a
grocery box?

Moth. Per. Whose child is that, any relation of yours?

Gamboge [*aside, Heaven forbid*]. I don't know whose child it
is.

Moth. Per. What is it doing here?

Gamboge. That is a question I fain would ask myself.

The Child. You need not whisper, say it out loud; I hear you;
I am in pursuit of Art culture. I read the criticisms and I came
to see if you were a true artist or a servile imitator—Were you a
true artist you would encourage me in my thirst for Art.

[*Exit* CHILD, *slamming door.*

Gamboge [*aside*]. I'd like to educate her with an old slipper.

Moth Per. I must go, now, but I shan't forget you—I know the
way an' I'll come real often—Good bye.

Gamboge [*bowing her to the door*]. Thanks, madame.

[*Exit* MOTHERLY PERSON.

Brown. By the way, Gamboge, that's a neat little thing, ye dog and child; quite in ye Dutch spirit and feeling. How one of my daughters would like that for her room. Is it ordered.

Gamboge. Yes, it is sold. [*Aside*] How I wish it was.

Brown. I'll tell you what I'll do, Gamboge: you paint me a first-rate picture, and I'll hang it up in our Queen Nancy living-room at my chateau; I will, indeed. You're no genius, Gamboge, and you haven't much talent, but you're no drone. There's a want of freedom in your handling, but you're an industrious fellow and I want to see you get on. Now you paint me some bit of sky and some green, or ye flock of sheep in ye thunder-storm, or ye Oriental sword dance—I leave ye motif to yourself, and if you do it *well*, I'll have your name put on ye frame. People will be sure to see it; we have so many visitors and it will bring you in orders. I'll drop in next week. Good-day and grammercy!

[*Exit* BROWN.

Young Bride. Mr. Gamboge, have you a little bit of carmine you don't want, just the tiniest little bit? I want to decorate an Etruscan vase with some Lady Washington geraniums, and I am too tired to go all the way down to Cobalt's to buy it.

Gamboge [*hands her a little tube*]. There is a trifle of it, madame.

Young Bride. Oh, thanks! I'm awfully obliged. Now, when you paint something *real sweet* I'll send some friends of mine to look at it. Good-bye. Wish I could stay longer, but my husband will be home and he is so lonely without me.   [*Exit* Y. B.

[GAMBOGE *closes door after* YOUNG BRIDE, *and turning around discovers* ÆSTHETIC MAIDEN *asleep on the sofa; looks up in embarrassment at the* WOMAN REPORTER, *who is scribbling in a note-book.*]

Woman Reporter. I guess I've got euough for three-quarters of a column. Can't you help me spin it out to a column, then I'll get five dollars for it.

Gamboge. If you would suggest anything, I might tell you what I know about it.

Woman R. Oh, anything about artists to fill up; any romantic incidents or cases of destitution. Is any painter going to the seaside or has he had an order from a rich man. Anybody in consumption, or going to be married, or going to Europe?

Gamboge. Yes, Chloral died last night.

Woman R. Consumption?

Gamboge. Yes, call it consumption.

Woman R. [*scribbling*] Go on; I've got that. I'm afraid you're tired. I won't keep you much longer. Tell me what sort of a painter Gizzard is, and I'll go.

Gamboge. What sort?

W. R. Yes, what is his style? Tell me what I had better say about his last picture; I haven't seen it, but I asked Vandyck and Vert Green, and now you, and I guess between you I can strike an average. What shall I call it—French or American?

Gamboge. Call it Franco-American, the newspapers have not used that word threadbare.

W. R. You do look tired. I wonder if you don't have your own trouble? I do. I tell you writing for the papers is no joke, and don't you just earn your money. Pay's good enough, but it's too slow. Before I jumped into this thing of writing on Art, I tried everything—wax flowers, whole art in one lesson, patent process; then I beaded parasols and did spatter-work and decalcomanie for a notion house; then I canvassed Picturesque America and Duplex Elliptic corsets, but I was getting into typhoid fever and my head was all of a whirl, and one day I was fagged out I got into a broker's office, where there was a lot of gentlemen, and I got Picturesque and the corsets all mixed up, and they thought I'd been drinking, but it was the fever coming on me. After that I was ill ten weeks; I got in the dollar store, and there it was nip and tuck, I couldn't get out of debt; so I thought I'd make a bold strike for the Spiritualists,—"seventh daughter of a seventh daughter; tells family secrets; reveals destinies; shows husband's photograph; eighth wonder of the world; Ladies, 50 cents; no Gents; ring the basement bell." I had an ad. all written out when I met a young fellow, foreman in printing office of the Fog Whistle, and says he to me, he says—why don't you write on Art, that's the latest dodge? O land, I says, I can't tell a chromeo from an Old Master. Yes, he says. Go to a second-hand shop and get a lot of old art catalogues by Ruskin and those fellows and read em up; so it reads well, that's all the papers care. And so I did, and in about a month I could tell which way the cat jumped as well as the next one, and I skipped out of that dollar store lively. I move now in tip-top society, and here I am.

Gamboge. IIow long did you say you had been writing on Art?

W. R. About a year,—but I must go, you're busy, ain't you?

Gamboge [*smiling*]. I have not had a chance to be busy. I have been interrupted so many times to-day.

W. R. Haven't you had your dinner yet? Don't be offended, I'm right out, I am. If you're short, I can lend you a couple of dollars.

Gamboge [*quickly*]. No, no, but I thank you,—I mean I have had no time to leave my studio.

W. R. Your wife's asleep; she believes in taking things easy; she's just right.

Gamboge. The lady is a perfect stranger to me. Would you— [*hesitatingly*] be good enough to wake her?

W. R. [*shaking* ÆSTHETIC MAIDEN]. Wake up, wake up, Mr. Gamboge wants to go to his dinner.

Æsthetic Maiden. Ah! I did but dream then. Methought I was in the Sistine chapel in Italy.

W. R. To be continued in our next. You had better finish your dream in your own boarding-house, and let this man have a rest. Good-bye, Mr. Gamboge; I am much obliged. Send you a copy of my Art article.   [*Exit* WOMAN REPORTER.

A. Maiden [*calling after W. R.*]. Woman, don't leave me alone, and here. How indiscreet of you. Wait for me. Adieu, Mr. Gamboge; forgive my discourteous haste.   [*Exit.*

Gamboge (*solemnly.*) Thank heaven, I am alone. I began to think I never should be (*changes his coat*). I am going to have a

new rule about visitors, either that or blow my brains out, that is
if I have any to blow out, which I am beginning to doubt.
Humph—Fog Whistle's impudence, I'll do him a picture when
he pays in advance for it. The D. E. Corset canvasser is a caution
for veterans, but she's an ornament to society compared with him.
Wonder what Moddle wanted so all of a sudden. There he is
now.

*Enter rough looking stranger who walks into the centre of the
studio and stares at the artist without speaking.*

Gamboge. Did you wish to see me?

Stranger. My name's Byles, Bill Byles, can you paint?

Gamboge. These are my works, Mr. Byles.

Byles [*contemptuously*]. I don't mean those jimcracks, the man
who has done my painting work has gone to Frisco, and I thought
may be I could get a painter feller like you, to do it well enough·
I wanted a sign painted. Could you do it?

Gamboge [*glancing nervously at the door*]. Yes, I can paint a
sign for you.

Byles. Now I don't want you to put any high art ruffles in it.
I want an oyster sign. Could you paint an oyster sign?

Gamboge [*faintly*]. Yes, I can paint an oyster sign. What
name? and how large is it to be?

Byles. No name at all—I want a border kinder fancy, of
oysters all around it, and three plates in the middle. Could you
paint an oyster plate?

Gamboge. Oh, yes.

Byles. Then I want you to paint on the plates, a raw, and a fry and a stew. Hold up, I only live a block off; couldn't I send you a raw and a fry and a stew every day until it is done. Don't you make no mistake—I won't dock it off your pay.

Gamboge [smiling]. Thanks, that would be a good idea, they would be of great use to me to paint from [*aside, " And to eat afterwards*].

Byles. And then in some nice, handy way, couldn't you paint a bottle of ketchup and some crackers and—do you think you could paint a plate of cold slaw?

Gamboge [trying not to smile]. If you were to send the cold slaw I think I could manage it.

Byles. I guess that's all; now bis is bis. What'll you take to paint a sign like that? Speak out, and no gander dancing.

Gamboge [timidly]. Would fifteen dollars be too much?

Byles. I'll give you twenty dollars if you do it bang up this week. Here's ten now—the balance on delivery. I'll send the lumber and oysters around in two shakes of a lamb's tail.

Gamboge. Thank you, sir, you are very prompt. I wish all my patrons were the same.

Byles. They ain't; you needn't tell me; I seed it in your face, quick as I came in. But I worked hard when I started in the business an' I can feel for a fellow who has small sales and no profits. Well, so long. Be good to yourself.

[*Exit.*

Gamboge [looks at ten dollar note, puts it in his vest pocket, does a caper about the room, then seats himself and laughs aloud]. Heaven tempers the wind to the shorn lamb. I'll never lose faith again; I'll ask Moddle to dine with me to-day, and to-morrow I'll feast on oysters. Oysterman you're a trump; the right and left bower and all the aces. [*Knocks on the wall.*]

Moddle's voice. Halloo.

Gamboge. Come in here, I want you.

Moddle's voice. All right.

Enter MODDLE.

Gamboge. Have you had your dinner?

Moddle. No, just going.

Gamboge. Dine with me. I have had an unexpected streak of luck, only a pot-boiler, but enough for present necessities. [*Loud knocking at the door.*] Whoever that is I'll say plump out that I can't stay, for I'm as hungry as fifteen bears. [*Opens door*].

Enter two MEN, *one with a large board, the other with a covered tray.*

1st man. Mr. Gamboge?

Gamboge. Yes.

1st man. This board is for you.

Gamboge. Put it here.

2nd man. Is your name Gamboge?

Gamboge. It is.

2d Man. This here tray of oysters is for you [*places tray on table*]—one box stew, one big fry, one dozen raw, crackers, ketchup, cold slaw, pepper sass, salt, pepper, mustard, knives, forks, spoons, plates, pumpkin pie, two pints of pale ale,—all right, sir?

Gamboge. All right, my fine fellow. [*aside*] Immensely all right.

Moddle [*whistling*]. You have done it, haven't you? You're a reckless fellow to squander your substance in this fashion. I did not understand that we were to dine here.

Gamboge [*aside*]. Neither did I; [*to* MODDLE] sit down while its hot. Nature abhors a vacuum, at least mine does.

[*They seat themselves.* GAMBOGE *helps his friend plentifully.*]

Moddle. Here's richness.

Gamboge. They *are* good.

Moddle. Good is not strong enough.

Gamboge. Why don't you eat? Here now, don't leave them to waste.

Moddle. Softly, Gam. I *was* hungry; all the same I haven't the stomach of an ostrich. I have been wildly impatient to tell you of the brilliant idea I have conceived for paying off old Brown. Its something in your line—now don't say no—its just a nice job for both of us, especially you; and Grasshopper and Cricket.

Gamboge. Grasshopper and Cricket?

Moddle. Even so, I have already talked it over with them and you never saw two such cases of inoculation in all your life, they're going into train at once.

Gamboge. Is it a conundrum? I hate conundrums.

Moddle. You want to pay off old Brown, don't you?

Gamboge. Don't I?

Moddle. Now as we've finished our dinner, lock the door and let us get to our work; you get at your sign; I know what that board is for—and I have some buttons to paint for a Yankee Notion house; so that we shall not be disturbed, write a card on the door and say we are out of town, for a few days.

Gamboge. Suppose we do it up in style. Here's a good sized card—[*writes, then reads aloud*] " Gone to dine with August Belmont; will return in five days." How's that?

Moddle. A stroke of genius.

Gamboge. Now what are you going to do with Brown—he was here to-day. Curse his impudence.

Moddle. I am going to marry his daughter.

Gamboge. Are you, indeed?

Moddle. I am, and *you* shall marry his daughter.

Gamboge. Oh, shall I? The same one?

Moddle. No, her sister.

Gamboge. Thank you, that is certainly a less startling way of putting it. Much obliged; small favors thankfully received, etc., you know the rest. But what's the plot?

Moddle. You know Brown's craze for objets d'art, as he calls them?

Gamboge. Slightly.

Moddle. And you may have caught a glimpse of his daughters' passion for the mediæval?

Gamboge. Rather.

Moddle. And you have heard that the family " collect."

Gamboge. A few.

Moddle. And you know they live in a barn ?

Gamboge. No, by Jove, I didn't. That's the latest news from the seat of war is it, well?

Moddle. Briefly then, you and I and our upstairs familiars must play a practical joke on them—you have the gift of gab—

Gamboge. Thank you.

Moddle. So you must be Dr. Bric-a-brac, a great collector. I will be your friend, an authority on old china, by name, Claude Kaolin ; we visit them with a cart load of curios—which I am sure two ingenious fellows as you and I—ahem—ought to be able to contrive. We will make them lively curiosities you know, and astonish the Browns, somewhat ; Grasshopper, Cricket and Stumps, you know, who will make the rafters of that barn ring—then in the midst of it we'll trump-up a charge against Brown for receiving stolen goods, and two mock policemen shall arrest the whole family. We in *propria personœ* appear in the nick of time—" The Rescue," " The Betrothal," and bless you my children and ring down the curtain to waltz time—Eh ?

Gamboge. It will take some thinking.

Moddle. And more talking. A few yards of rubber cloth, some pins and some good accidents of color, and we can make anything in the market from a giant in Satsuma to a mummy in old Bronze.

Gamboge. Success to your plan.

Moddle. Our plan, if you please.

Gamboge. Success to our plan, then, here's to our future bride and brother-in-law, and confusion to their dad.

[*They touch the empty glasses.*]

END OF ACT I.

ACT II. HIGH ART—IN THE BARN BEAUTIFUL.

SCENE I.—*Interior of a barn, in the suburbs of a city, appointed in the Eastlake, Rococo, Mediæval, Queen Nancy style; the* MISSES ALFRESCO DADO *and* MAUD CASHMERE BOUQUET BROWN, *seated at embroidery and pottery painting; two ankles of their handmaiden* COSETTE *appear beneath the portière which divides the culinary department from the " living room." Incidental music during this act, by* COSETTE, *addicted to smashing dishes ; an inquisitive rooster, a crow, and a cow in the distance.*

Enter MISS ALHAMBRA FRIEZE.

Alhambra. I had such a time to find your house—barn—chateau, I mean. I am *so* glad to see you. How perfectly exquisite your new home is. It is *just* charming. It makes me think of dear, darling Italy.

Alfresco [*kissing her in rapture*]. You're just one naughty girl for not coming to us before.

Maud. Indeed you are. We have been *pining* to see you. We have so much to tell you.

Alfresco. I knew you would like our house. Is not this a symphony in homes?   [*Music by* COSETTE *and the cow.*]

Alhambra. I *have* been neglectful, but I am coming real often now. What a little paradise! So æsthetic! so artistic! It makes me think of a grand chord in one of Wagner's hymns or a poem by Browning. Don't you feel as if you were in heaven?

Alfresco. Yes, Alhambra, we are sweetly tranquil [*noise of wash-ing dishes is heard behind the mediæval hangings*]; our lives are as simple and primitive as the ancient Greeks. No bustle, no din of the hollow world [COSETTE *smashes a plate*], no bickerings no heart-burnings, such as are felt by those who live a fashionable life, do we know. We revel in the art works of the mighty Past. We commune daily with the spirits of the masters of the Middle Ages. Oh, how I wish it were the Middle Ages now, Alhambra. But we are cheerful; we do not repine; but patiently hope that the time may come when something worthy the name of Art shall be done in this, our own country. Cosette, our maid; Angelico Benvenuto Cellini, our page, attend to our wants, which are few and simple. At night we gather about our sacred tripod and papa reads to us his criticisms, or from some fragmentary paper he may have written during the day to elevate American Art.

Alhambra. Your embroidery is too lovely for anything. Is it your own design?

Alfresco. Yes, that is to say, almost my own design. I got it in part from a funeral pall of the Elizabethan age. I am going to have it made up for a window bench, if in the neighborhood I can find a carpenter with a feeling for his business. Even now Ben-venuto is looking for one for me.

Alhambra. What a lovely bust! And how beautifully that tor-chon lace ruffle looks around its neck !

Alfresco. I am glad you like it, dear. It is a genuine antique. That is just the corner for a bust—the toned white of the marble against the blue necktie sympathizes with our rather severe scheme of color, papa thinks.

Enter A. B. C. BAXTER, *the page.*

Alfresco. Speak, Benvenuto.

Ben [*grinning*]. Couldn't fin' no Midinville carpenter, Mis' Frisker, dar ain't none ob dat ar in de town.

Alfresco. You have not searched diligently. Go, ask at the post office.

Ben. I dun went dar.

Alfresco. Did you inquire at the mill?

Ben. Yes, Mis' Frisker, an de miller's wife said she nebber heard ob no mechanic ob dat style.

Alfresco. Oh, the ignorance of the masses! I told you to say of the Middle Ages.

Ben. Yes, Mis' Frisker, I done said dat it peared like how you wanted a middle-aged carpenter, an' she tole me to ax you if a young man ob twenty-five years wouldn't suit you?

Maud. There, go to your duties, stupid minion. Alfresco, my sister, we must needs wait until we can pick up something in London or Paris or Vienna.

Alfresco. Don't loiter, Benvenuto; if you have nothing else to do, go to Cosette and paste some tasteful chromos on the Hispano-Moresque pie-plates your master brought from the museum yesterday. [*Exit* BENVENUTO.

Alhambra. I do so want to get an ecclesiastic chair for my boudoir. I have hunted all over the city for it and I have been in all the artistic second-hand shops without success.

Maud. You can get it at Fraction's.

Alhambra. No, dear, I tried; they are bought up. Mr. Fraction said he could make a *fortune* if he could supply the demand for ecclesiastic chairs.

Alfresco. Must it be second-hand, Alhambra, dear?

Alhambra [*reproachfully*]. Yes, of course.

Alfresco. Then, if I were you, I would have it made to order. You can get any second-hand bargain duplicated; no one could ever tell that it was new if well done. You know Judge Plankdown's cabinet of rare Dutch marquetry of the 16th century, Fraction made that for him in six weeks, brass clasps and all.

Alhambra. But where is Connie, all this time, and how is her *affaire tendre* progressing?

Alfresco. O, Connie is such a trial to us; she nearly worries our lives out with her irreverence for Art. She ridicules everything; our artistic home, our artistic labor and our artistic hopes. You know Dr. Bricabrac and Mr. Kaolin, the great connoisseurs?

Alhambra. I haven't met them, but I have heard of them, and am wild to be introduced.

Alfresco. Give me that pleasure, they are valued friends of ours : but I was about to say that Connie treats them very rudely, and she actually told them she was going to be married, that she might live among sane people once more.

Maud. Where is she? I wish her to go buy some crewels for me. [*Calls*] "Connie."

[*Connie's voice behind the portière*] I'm coming [*pettishly*].

Enter in riding habit.

Alfresco. Where are you going?

Connie. Going for a gallop with Dr. Sam. How d'y do, Miss Frieze? How's the Middle Ages at your house?

Alfresco. Connie, will you ever stop your slang? I do wish you would be more dignified and not spend all your time riding over the village; people will think it very strange of papa to allow his youngest child to wander about alone.

Connie. That isn't the only thing that the people in these diggings think strange. This ranche of ours is the talk of the place. Only this morning I heard we were traveling Gipsies, and the Winslow's gardener asked Cosette if there was madness in our family.

Alfresco. There have been noble sufferers for the cause of Art before us. *We* can afford to treat the sneers of common people with lofty contempt. What other solace do you need than the study of Egyptian pottery? What other society than your embroidery frame and your Mediæval crewel samplers?

Connie. I'm not going to live in a junk shop for the sake of Art or anything else, nor spend my time sewing crazy dandelions on kitchen toweling, nor pasting chromos on frying pans, nor any high or low art moonshine. I admire pretty things and love pictures and I can tell an engraving from an oil painting, which is more than half your art critics can do, but I don't want to have "Art" dinned into my ears morning, noon and night.

Maud. Alfresco, dear, let her alone, she will never be like the rest of us, no, not if she lives till doomsday.

Connie. I don't want to be. I am going to marry a man with a reputation to sustain and it won't help him if it gets abroad that he is going to marry into a crazy family.

Alhambra. Why, Connie, how unkind of you.

Connie. They may as well hear it from me as from strangers. Every time we go out we are stared at as if we were bedlamites, and I am getting tired of it.

Alfresco. Dr. Sam is at the bottom of this. It is because of his influence that you are so impertinent; I know he dislikes us, but if you had any family pride you would resent his insolent allusions to our artistic home.

Connie. He doesn't dislike you.

Enter DR. SAM.

Dr. Sam. Indeed I do not dislike you, Alfresco, I think you and Maud and my Connie are the loveliest girls in America and I would do anything to prove my regard for you—that is to say, I would do anything in reason, but I can't neglect my patients for the Middle Ages, and I couldn't mix the Mediæval medicines with nineteenth century doses—upon my word, I could not. I'm a radical and all my patients are uncompromisingly of this day of

their own. I don't think I could get one of them to take a Queen
Anne pill or an Elizabethan mustard plaster to save my life. They
would dismiss me first, and if my practice is ruined Connie and I
can't get married. [*Sits down on a plaque which* MAUD *has painted
and transfers the design to his white trousers.*] Oh, the dev— I
beg your pardon. Here's a nice mess.

Connie. Oh plague take your old pottery! Look at my Sam's
trousers. [*Begins to cry.*]

Maud [*sobbing*]. Well, what did he sit down on my early Italian
plaque for—he's just ruined it!

Dr. Sam. Oh, dear, it is going through. Is it poison?

Maud. No, I just wish it was [*sobbing*].

Alfresco. Don't cry, Maud, don't cry. Dr. Sam you're a brute.

Dr. Sam. Alfresco Dado Brown, I am behaving like an angel;
look at my trousers!

Alfresco. Look at poor Maud's plaque!

Dr. Sam. Look at my trousers!

Connie. Come, Sam dear, I'll wash it off with benzine. Don't
you ever go near their horrid old paint pots again. Come, Sam.

Dr. Sam. Good bye, ladies. Destiny and my trousers call me
hence. Adieu Miss Frieze; when you find yourself venting the
holy emotions of your soul in early Italian maiolica—think of my
trousers.　　　　　　　　　　　　[*Exit* CONNIE *and* DR. SAM.

Enter BEN.

Ben. Mis' Frisker the two gemmen what brings de hot objecks are coming up de road in a carriage, an' deys got a truck follerin 'em.

Alfresco. I'm so glad. Bathe your eyes Maud; don't go Alhambra, Dr. Bricabrac and his friend are coming, you must stay and see the curios he is going to lend us while his new museum is being built. Some of them are priceless. Benvenuto, attend the door. [*Exit* BEN.

Enter DR. BRICABRAC *and* KAOLIN.

Bric. Ah, ladies, I am delighted to greet you once more, this is the happiest picture I have ever seen in my life, your home is like a dream of the past, setting off your beauty, like chased gold does the gem. Are you all quite well? Ah, this is your valued friend Miss Frieze? Permit me to introduce my friend, Mr. Kaolin; Claude, this is Miss Frieze of whom you have heard.

Miss F. Delighted to meet you, sir.

Kaolin. The pleasure is mine, madame.

Dr. B. I have brought the curios which you were so appreciative as to wish to see, and if you think they will fill a void in your gentle souls until my museum is finished, I will gladly leave them with you. Ah—shall we go over the catalogue at once.

Alfresco. Please do, dear doctor.

Maud. By all means, doctor.

Dr. B. My servant and Benvenuto shall bring them to me as I read from my catalogue. The first is a pre-Raphaelite textile Fabric, No. 3007. [*Produces "basket" bed-quilt.*]

Chorus. How sweet! How boldly designed!

Dr. B. [*reads*]. No. 4231, M, Night cap of an early Dutch painter. [*Produces a bottle of Schiedam Schnapps.*]

Chorus. Ah, indeed.

Alfresco. There is something so instructive in the customs of that quaint people.

Dr. B. [*reads*]. No. 7,444 is, pre-historic cleansing utensil from the recent excavation in Ohio. [*Exhibits a white-wash brush, much worn.*]

Chorus. Ah, indeed.

Alfresco. Our country has a great unwritten history.

Dr. B. No. 7,346 1, An Anglo-Hibernian vegetable masher. [*Exhibits Kehoe club.*]

Chorus. Ah, indeed.

Dr. B. No. 1,643,020, n, A genuine Greek Cratere. [*Produces a basket-covered demijohn.*]

Chorus. Ah, indeed. Isn't it sweet?

Dr. B. [*aside*]. Yes, there's sugar in it.

Kaolin [*aside*]. And it's the genuine crather too.

Dr. B. [*reads*]. No. 3000, an Athenian sauté pan.

Chorus. Ah, indeed. My gracious!

Alfresco. Is it not rather deep for a sauté pan? At our cooking class we don't use one more than four inches deep.

Dr. B. Ah, yes, but allow me to explain. This shape was suggested to an Athenian chêf by a Phœnician cook who had been employed in the kitchen of the Pharoahs. It was used to prepare a dish of which afterwards the Greeks became inordinately fond.

They let a few ounces of butter brown in the pan and then put in a layer of onions, then a porter-house steak, and finally a double layer of onions; in fact, my dear Miss Brown, it was the ancient method of preparing the pastoral dish—the classic beefsteak smothered in onions.

Alfresco [*breathing freely and long*]. I am so glad I know. I must make note of it for our cooking class.

Enter BEN *and* MURPHY *with large curio.*

Dr. B. Gently Ben, gently, easy Murphy, easy my man. This my friends, No. 11,078, F. is an Egyptian mummy, age one hundred thousand years.

[*Exit* BEN *and* MURPHY.

Alfresco. Isn't it a little thing? I thought they were large. Poor Mummy. Heartless Time, to have caused you to shrink thus.

Mummy [*aside*]. Little! Shrunk! It is a wonder there is anything left of me after the shaking I got in that wagon!

Enter BEN *and* MURPHY.

Dr. B. Steady men, be careful. Be careful, that bit of old egg shell china cost me a pretty penny. Should feel awfully grieved if you broke any part of it.

Bit of old China [*aside*]. So should I.

Dr. B. [*reads*]. No. 8,642, Y. a large Chinese Mandarin, portrait figure of Jim-lung-jam-lee, a wealthy potentate, contemporary with Confucius.

Alfresco. Oh, what an amusing creature, I never saw one so large before. It is almost life-size. Can it rock itself? [*Attempts to move the Mandarin, thereby putting the wooden bowl in which it is placed, in motion.*]

Alhambra [*touching it*]. It looks just as if it could speak if it had a mind to.

Maud. Please rock it Dr. Bricabrac.

Dr. B. Certainly. Rock-a-by, Mandy. [*Aside to the bit of China*]. If you spread out you arms, Cricket, I'll thrash you.

Alfresco. Let me! Don't it go nice! I could just rock you all day, you funny old curio. [*Curio winks at her.*] Oh, my dear! oh doctor! what is the matter with its eyes?

Dr. B. It is in a bad light. Allow me to move it here. [*Aside to the bit of china*]. Now, Cricket, behave yourself, or I'll give you Jessie. It isn't time for you to cut up your shines yet.

Enter BEN *and* MURPHY *with a statue.*

Dr. B. Easy my lads, steady now. Very careful Murphy, put it on the pedestal. The last and best. No. 5,270. An old Greek marble. "Innocence sucking its thumb," sculptor unknown. It is supposed to have been discovered by a Dutch general in a vast plain, which legend assigned as the original Garden of Eden. It has been the subject of much varied and learned criticism and was probably executed when Greek art was in its decline.

Bit of old China [*aside to statue*]. If you're an old marble, I spose I'm a chiny alley.

Dr. B. [*aside*]. Cricket, behave yourself.

Alfresco. Is it not a gem? How shall we ever thank you, doctor?

Maud. Indeed, doctor, I wish we could thank you sufficiently but words are weak to express our joy.

Alfresco. How happy we shall be! I'll never be melancholy again, for with those wonderful *objets d' art* about me I shall have a wealth of thought which will absorb my inmost spirit the long days to come. Time cannot pall or annoy with these about me. I shall commune with them and the masters which bade them be and endure, and I shall be happy.

Kaolin [*aside*]. If she isn't, it won't be Cricket's fault.

Alfresco. But while we are admiring our new possessions, we are forgetting your creature comforts. You must be hungry after your long drive. Benvenuto shall bring the bread and wine. What! Ho! Without there! Who waits! [*Stops in confusion and presses her hand over her brow.*] I—I—really don't know how it is, but occasionally I get in this manner of speaking. In fact, ever since we have occupied our new home, I seem to live in the middle ages and relapse into the phraseology of olden time. I think it must be the effect of the new curios.

Maud. And so does papa. Don't you remember, dear, it was only the other night when Cosette surprised papa by snuffing the candle into the salad instead of the tray, he exclaimed, "By my Hali-dame, wench," and sometimes he says, "Grammercy," he declares he cannot help it.

Enter BEN. *with tea, wine and fruit. The* MISSES BROWN *press their guests to partake of the food.*

Kaolin. What a wonderful eye for color you ladies have. The grouping on the tea table is as admirable a symphonic treatment as I have ever seen.

Dr. B. And the subjective tones of the bread and butter against the green plate is a marriage of sweet hues.

Maud. Oh, doctor, you talk *just* like one of papa's *Art* articles.

Dr. B. Now really Miss Brown, that *is* high praise indeed, it is a bonus of honor which my modesty will not permit me to appropriate. I never *could* talk like your respected father. [*Aside.*] Heaven forbid !

Alhambra [*in terror*]. Oh--oh—ouch!

Alfresco and Maud. What is the matter, Alhambra, dear?

Alhambra. Some horrid creature is in this apple and has stung me in the mouth. Oh my goodness how it hurts! Do you think it will swell?

Alfresco [*falteringly*]. I am afraid it is the pins which I put in the little bows of blue ribbon to decorate them; the glue would not stick and I put a pin through the centre of the bow. I am *so* sorry it ran in your mouth,—but don't you think it a pretty idea? I got it from reading a criticism of papa's on the English water-colorists. It seemed to me that the apples were too warm a red and I thought a little pale blue ribbon would tone it down; but blue is such a difficult color to handle.

Dr. B. [*aside*]. Darling Alfresco, may I not see you alone for two fleeting moments?

Alfresco [*aside*]. I shall try to get rid of Alhambra, and sister and Mr. Kaolin will be glad to walk out in the garden together.

Dr. B. [*aside*]. Do, my angel.

Alfresco. Alhambra, dear, I fear your poor, dear mouth is swelling. I am so sorry for you, but it is looking dreadfully.

Alhambra. Oh, is it? What shall I do?

Dr. B. If you were at home, a piece of cold raw beef laid on it would remove the swelling.

Alhambra. Then I must go at once. No, dear, I really can't stay any longer; I must go home or I shall be a fright. I'll come soon again. Good-bye dear. [*Kisses the* MISSES BROWN *and makes a feint of kissing* DR. B.; *discovers her mistake and retires in confusion.*] Oh, dear, I am so ill I don't know what I am doing.   [*Exit* AL. b.

[BRIC. *and* ALFRESCO, MR. KAOLIN *and* MAUD *stand in couples conversing in a low tone, the curios meanwhile are helping themselves to the food with relish and pantomime.*]

Alfresco. Maud, dear.

Maud. Sister mine.

Alfresco. Don't you think Mr. Kaolin would like to see our dear old apple trees?

Maud. Claude, do you love apple trees?

Kaolin. Dearest Maud, I adore them,—next to you.

Maud. Shall we go for a walk then?

Kaolin. With all my heart.   [*Exit* MAUD *and* KAOLIN, *L. D.*

Dr. B. My darling Alfresco, do you truly love me?

Alfresco. Yes, my very own, you know I do.

Dr. B. I would fain believe you, but you have known me so

short a time, and this is a deceitful world,—at least I have found
it so, and sometimes the fear haunts me that my vanity expects too
much, and that my dear little duck of a decorator, my sweet
mignonne pottery putterer, my macrame fringed cherub, my fond-
est stork embroidered anti-macassar, my precious darling decalcomanie, my iridescent Venitian glass goblet, my cameo, my intag-
lio, my whole catalogue of gems, loves me for my curios and not
for myself; but you do love me, sweetheart, don't you? Say it
again. Say to me, that if I were only a poor artist with five thousand a year, and had not a museum to my name, nor a bit of early
Italian maiolica to my back, nor the shadow of an Egyptian
mummy to foster an art-atmosphere in our home, but only my
heart to love you, my eyes to adore you, and my hands to work
for you, and keep your own like white rose petals, and my broad
breast for you to rest upon, and keep your dear little tootsy-
wapsies from the cold, cold ground, would my sweet darling lovey
dovey decorated pre-Raphaelite love me then, would her?

Alfresco. Ah, my own, my very, veriest own, my chosen Bricabrac, collector of collectors, more steadfast than *Cloisneé*, more
precious than "old blue,"—how the very name thrills me with
fond association. Yes, even if I found you had deceived me, that
instead of being a great connoisseur I were to find in you a mere
worldling, a merchant millionaire, after what has transpired, I
should love you and be your wife.

Dr. B. Oh, bliss.   [*They embrace.*]

Alfresco [*disengaging herself*]. But now let me show you the little dower I am going to bring you, the things I have made for our new home with my very own hands. Help me to lift this box, dearest.

Dr. B. Ah, this is my charge.

[*Lifts chest to centre of stage. Alfresco opens it.*]

Alfresco. Here is your smoking cap and wrapper, trimmed with macrame lace, and here is an inlaid clothes pole for the kitchen, and here is a cartoon—a design for the iron gate of a private menagerie, when we can afford one,—and here are some bits of old china, I did them; and here is a set of embroidered cheese cloths to dust the curios,—and here—don't blush—I have taken some liberty with your wardrobe and have made you some shirts, —that is to say, I bought them made, but decorated them myself; you will think of me when you wear them, won't you, dear? [*Spreads out the decorated shirt.*] Don't you think the sunflower design on the front bold and original?

Dr. B. I do indeed, dear. I am sure it will create a sensation on the avenue. [*Aside*] Oh, Lord.

Alfresco. I knew you would admire it. And I have a set of designs here for our best dinner dishes, each represents the rise and fall of every art of every country, and in the middle I have entwined our monograms, and here's a little place I have left bare for our crest,—that is if we can look up our genealogy and get one. I had rather find one from *the* Browns in ancient history than have one made at Tiffany's for us. But, dearest, haven't you a coat-of-arms in your family? We really must have one.

Dr. B. Oh, yes; our family were distinguished in the early Irish wars; on the distaff side they were all Borhues, and the coat of arms was a green field bearing on it a shillaly rampant.

Alfresco. How delightful! Won't you hunt it up for us, like a dear? I'd just love to have it on our coupe, we won't have a *coupé*—we'll have a sweet low-backed car, shan't we?

Dr. B. It would be distractingly picturesque, certainly.

Alfresco. And we'll have a Shillaly Rampant blazoned on each side,—why that reminds me—I think I have some family documents belonging to you; you dropped it out of your pocket-book when you were here last. It is *so* quaint and queer. I showed it to Maud, and she said, she thought if we took it to an Oriental scholar he could decipher it for us, but I feared you might not like it, and thought it better to ask you to explain it to me.

Dr. B. [*absently*]. You were a thoughtful darling. I don't remember losing any hieroglyphic paper.

Alfresco [*produces little folded paper*]. First, there is three curious round things like pills, then there's a dash and some dots, and something that looks like "doll" and the "250," and then beneath it says, "not answerable in case of fire, moth or robbery," —why what's the matter?

Dr. Bric [*taking paper from her*]. Yes it is—it is—it's a family paper, you were quite right, it is a family paper and was given me by my uncle [*aside, Uncle Simpson*].

Alfresco. I thought it was a label from some rare curio.

Mr. Bric. You are gifted with divination my sweetest—it is—

[*aside*] It is the ticket of my dress coat, precious rare, I have not seen it for nearly a year.

Alfresco. Won't you tell me what it means? You ought to have no secrets from me.

Dr. Bric [*desperately*]. Well, daughter of Eve, you see these three round things are the emblems, or ancient marks of the great de Medicis, and in reality mean pills, for the family were renowned centuries ago for their discoveries in medicine. [*Aside*] How shall I get out of this? [*Noise at the door. Alfresco disengaging herself from Dr. Bricabrac's arms.*]

Alfresco. Oh, pshaw, there comes Maud and Mr. Kaolin and I have not said half what I intended to say to you.

Dr. B. How stupid of them. [*Aside*] Thank fortune!

Enter MAUD *and* KAOLIN.

Maud. You have only ten minutes to catch the train! Oh how quickly the afternoon has gone.

Dr. Bric. Really, is it so late? Then we must tear ourselves away. Good bye, *au revoir.* [*Kisses Alfresco's hand.*]

[*Exit* BRIC *and* KAOLIN.

[*Curios who have been capering about, run hurriedly to their places ; the* MUMMY *mounts the pedestal, the* MANDARIN *leans against the bust in the corner, while the* GREEK STATUE *crouches in the* MANDARIN'S *bowl.*

Alfresco. I think Dr. Bricabrac is the greatest connoisseur living.

Maud. In curios, yes, but of old china and maiolica, I think

Mr. Kaolin is one man in all the nineteenth century—I am perfectly happy to-day [*sighs*].

Alfresco. So am I [*sighs*].

Maud. How glad Papa will be when he sees our new possessions! Why, there is the dear Pater now.

Brown. My darling, my first born Alfresco, my lady Maud. But where is my little Arch-Rebel- Consuelo Renaissance?

Maud. Out riding with her doctor Sam, *as usual.*

Alfresco. Papa, dear, you can't guess what has happened. Now shut your eyes— No don't open your mouth— Shut your eyes. Now turn around. Now then, what do you think of this?

Brown. What do I see?

Alfresco. Doctor Bricabrac brought them—wasn't it lovely of him? See that Mummy! [*Points to* MUMMY *who has posed à la Col. Sellers.*]

Brown [*in a rapture*]. But this is grand! my dears, I take this as very friendly on the part of my friend Bricabrac, he has behaved handsomely, he has indeed. What power there is in that brow, in that um—um—marble, in ye um—ye an—in fact see how carefully ye color is worked up in ye bit of old china, doubtless by some celestial prehistoric artist, equal to Potta-Rubbia of Italy. And that a—um—that ah—*objet d' art* is ye figure-head of ye ancient bucaneer—I doubt not—

Alfresco [*aside*]. Why they look awfully queer some how, don't they to you Maud?

Maud [*aside*]. What did you say, dear?   I was thinking of Claud Kaolin.

Brown [*attitudinizing*]. Alfresco, hear me—that, *that* is ye only mummy I ever saw which struck me as being genuine.   Alfresco, Maud, my children, it was a glad day for me when it darkened—came beneath my humble rooftree.   Oh, you thing of old, you corpse of an ancient king—(probably)—you friend of ye Pharaohs and contemporary of dead and gone monarchs of mighty Egypt. Sharer of ye mystic secrets of ye sphynx, of that grandest of all conundrums—ye pyramids! Would you could speak now, and tell us of your own age, and put this frivolous time of ours to shame!   [*A loud knocking at the door.*]

Brown. What, ho! Benvenuto! Approach ye portal and bid him who waits *salve*, and *cave canem.*

Enter two POLICEMEN.

Brown. What would ye?

1st Policeman. Is your name Brown?

Brown. It is—sirrah.

1st Policeman [*drawing paper from his coat*]. You must come with me; you're my prisoner.

Brown. Marry fellow, what do ye mean?

1st Policeman. Now stash your gab—you're going up on three counts.

Alfresco. Ah! [*In terror.*]

Maud. Oh Papa! [*Sobbing.*]

Brown [*aroused to indignation and the American language*].

Hush girls! How dare you intrude upon me—I am a simple gentleman. [IST POLICEMAN *winks at* 2D POLICEMAN *and taps his head significantly.*] And I am the art critic of the *Fog Whistle—*

1st. Policeman. Now you needn't say anything to criminate yourself, but I'd like to know how much you expect to make out of the shady little plant you're on now.

Brown. "Plant," fellow, what does this insolence mean?

1st. Policeman. Don't try that on—it's too thin. I've had my eye on you for a long time, and thought you'd need my professional services; now are you coming peaceable, or shall I clap on the bracelets?

Brown. I demand to know of what I am accused.

2d Policeman. Tell him Billy.

1st Policeman. Receiving stolen goods. Harboring two escaped lunatics—these young women here—they go up with you, and vagrancy.

Brown. But my good man, you are mistaken, I assure you, we are a quiet family. I am an art critic—

1st Policeman. Didn't I tell you not to give yourself away? Now I'd advise you to stop chinnin' or you'll make things worse. We have our theory about you worked out fine.

Brown. I will give bail—come with me and I will give you security for my appearance at any time the law may demand, but now it is late, and I would be rid of you.

1st Policeman. Much obliged, but that won't work. We won't take any bail, its too late, and to-day's Saturday. You'll have to make the best of it in the jug until your case is tried next week. So come along—get your bunnits young women. Come along !

[*Lays his hand on Brown's shoulder.*]

Alfresco. Don't you dare touch my father. He is innocent. I call the angels to witness !

1st Policeman. Well young woman, if you can supeny them angels when your trial comes off, you'll score one for the Brown case, but now you are all coming along with me.

Maud. And leave our home !

Alfresco. Our sweet home, our own artistic paradise !

Brown. Our vine and fig tree !

1st Policeman. Don't feel bad old man, your vine and fig trees are comin' too, I have got a warrant for three of 'em. [*Seizes curios, who struggle ; the* MUMMY *tries to crawl under the portière. The* BROWNS *stare at them in consternation.*]

Brown. I am not mad—no, no, not mad. [*Tears his hair.*]

1st Policeman. Well, your neighbors wouldn't swear to that.

[*Seizes Brown.*]

Alfresco. Help—I die !

[*Swoons and is caught by the* MANDARIN.]

Maud. Oh my sister, I die with you !

[*Swoons and is caught by the* STATUE.]

Brown. My chield, my chield. [*Swoons and is caught by the* MUMMY, *who poses a la Col. Sellers.* COSETTE *smashing dishes as curtain falls.*]

END OF ACT II.

ACT III. HOME—IN A COTTAGE.

SCENE.—*Tastefully furnished drawing-room in the Gray Cottage, the residence of* DR. FLOYD.

Enter GAMBOGE, *followed by* MODDLE.

Moddle. Oh Gam, I'm a brute, I'm a brute!

Gamboge. And I'm another.

Moddle. Yes, we're both brutes.

Gamboge. But for all that, don't you go spoiling what we have done with your sentimental notions of justice. It's done, and can't be helped, and tho' I can't say that I altogether approve of what we did, the end partly reconciles me to the means. Maud and Alfresco were two very silly girls, for all their loveliness, and we have cured them; their father, begging their pardon, was an infernal ass; but now it is to be hoped that he has given up for all time his profession of making fools of others as he has been doing with his papers on art (*Poor Art!*). Viewing it in a pecuniary light, he had interfered with our means of obtaining our living—I do not believe there was any bitterness in the revenge we took upon him though I am afraid we frightened the girls.

Moddle. By Jove, Gam, I was frightened too, when I saw her lying like a dead lily in the arms of the bit of old china. Fortunately the rag carpets and rugs were thick.

Gamboge. But—ha! ha!—how the old fellow did beam upon us when we appeared in our own identity, as the trio were recovering from their swoon !

Moddle. And how he swallowed the story of our being near the barn beautiful sketching, and heard cries of distress and hastened to their rescue !

Gamboge. And how important a person I became in Brown's eyes when I told him I had influence with the police, and would be responsible for their appearance until he could get bail—but poor Alfresco, my heart misgave me when I saw her fainting in Cricket's arms !

Moddle. How well the little beggars played their parts !

Gamboge. Not to mention the talent of the big beggars, eh, Moddle ?

Moddle. As far as that was concerned, it all went off like a play, especially when we had to change our clothes.

Gamboge. Well then, as I said, let well enough alone. We courted the girls for spite, we are going to marry them for love— Maud hates Kaolin, the scamp, but adores Moddle, her preserver. Alfresco detests Bricabrac the impostor, but has promised to intrust her happiness into the keeping of Raphael Gamboge, the poor artist. I know they both have spirit, and I for one, am not so sick of self love, thank Heaven, as to believe her love for me now could make her forget my conduct to her then, and grant me a full pardon. But she needed a lesson ; they both did, and Brown, like a sensible man, has quit writing on art, of which he knows nothing, and has gone into manufacturing Macramé lace, for which, I admit, he has some talent, in fact—

Moddle. All's well, that ends well.

Gamboge. Ah, but here's the rub. We have not yet got to the end. Now I was about to propose this poser to you. What are we going to live on when we get married? But softly, here comes Mrs. Doctor Sam.

Enter MRS. DR. SAM FLOYD, *formerly* MISS CONNIE BROWN.

Mrs. Floyd. I am so glad to see you, alone for once. I have been trying to get a word with you two alone, ever since we returned from our wedding tour, for I must thank you for your efforts in persuading my misguided family to leave that detestable barn. What magic have you about you? How did you accomplish it? I ask the doctor, but he invariably replies, "Riddles, Connie, I know no more than you do." But come to confession, now, and tell me, how did you go about it?

Gamboge. Why really, Mrs. Floyd, you know we were in the neighborhood when they were in that scrape, and it was our duty to help them, which we did, and since then a more amiable feeling has been established between your father and ourselves.

Mrs. Floyd. Yes, I know, papa used to be severe on your pictures. I always thought them lovely, and it was so generous of you to get him out of that scrape, when by leaving him alone, you might have had revenge by seeing the disgraceful story in the papers. But I don't think papa really meant any harm by his art-writing, only he was fond of scribbling and it gave the whole family a sort of swagger you know.

Enter DOCTOR SAM FLOYD.

Doctor Sam [*interrupting*]. Mustn't say swagger, Connie dear. What are you all talking about?

Mrs. Floyd. Well, I mean it gave us a sort of air, to be pointed out as the daughters of a great art-critic, and sometimes papa got beautiful pictures from some of the artists of whose work he wrote, and that of course, was very nice.

Gamboge. I am sure it was an easy way of adding to his collection. [*Exchanges looks with Moddle.*]

Mrs. Floyd. And sometimes the artists would send him pictures before he wrote about them, so he must have had his admirers among your profession.

Doctor Floyd. And were they good, or bad pictures?

Mrs. Floyd. Why as it happened, they were all good, for papa puffed them all, and if they were big he wrote a half column each about them. But here are the girls.

Enter ALFRESCO *and* MAUD BROWN.

Mrs. Floyd. You are just in time Allie. I was telling Mr. Gamboge about a perfect symphony of a barn there is to let.

Alfresco. Now, Connie, will you please stop. You promised you would not say anything more about it.

Mrs. Floyd. Stop what, Allie, I was only telling my brother-in-law to be, of a chance to get a mediæval interior at a bargain.

Maud. Please, Connie, stop.

Mrs. Floyd. Why Doctor Sam, did you ever know two such ungrateful girls in all your life? Here I am offering to do all I can to aid them by my six weeks experience as a wife and housekeeper, and they look as if they were about to cry, and you sit there and see your lawful wife abused and don't interfere. Defend your altars and your fires and my dignity, Sam, tell them they must treat me with respect under your roof even if it is not shingled with early Dutch tiles.

Alfresco. Will you ever keep still about that barn. I *hate* barns.

Maud. So do I.

Moddle. I don't.

Gamboge. I don't either.

Mrs. Floyd. I used to, but I don't now, for its no end of fun to think of the sport that was carried on under that roof. When that horrid old Bricabrac used to call on Allie, and talk about Egyptian pottery and Hindoo rice plaques, I used to get behind the portière and make Cosette rattle the dishes, and once I made her fry some onions to see if I could not drive them out that way.

Alfresco. Won't you please, brother Sam, coax her to hold her tongue. I have eaten humble pie enough and am perfectly willing that my husband shall have a home utterly devoid of ornament, if he pleases.

Gamboge. Your husband is going to let his wife furnish her house to suit herself.

Mrs. Floyd. Your barn beautiful, you mean.

Doctor Sam. Connie, you little witch—I shall have to punish you—have either of you two ladies such a thing as a silver and Niello Damascened bowie-knife about you?

Alfresco. Sam, you're as bad as she is. Let us change the subject.

Doctor Sam. With all my heart—by the way, if it is not an impertinent question, when are you four people going to be married?

Moddle. Why the fact is—[*hesitates*].

Gamboge. The fact is—[*hesitates*].

Maud. Oh, dear, I wish I was rich!

Doctor Floyd. So do I, Maud, but what has that got to do with my question?

Moddle. Why you see—

Gamboge. The fact is, we have not got any money. I have pictures, and Moddle has got statuary, but they won't do us any good until we can turn them into dollars and cents. To come down to stern facts, what with the twaddle in the newspapers and the twaddle out of the newspapers, an American artist can't sell a picture unless he goes to Europe to do it, for rich people who are weak enough to be led by everything they see in print, had rather refuse to buy what their own innate good taste would lead them to purchase, than not put child-like faith in flimsy newspaper articles on Art, and so the "tolerably well to do" people buy chromos, and the artists starve.

Alfresco. Could not we live in the studio and save renting a house?

Gamboge. No, dearest, there would be no economy in that mixture.

Alfresco. Couldn't we help you in some way? I could do crewel work and sell it and—

Maud. And I could pose for Ralph.

Doctor Floyd. I wish I were rich enough to buy pictures and statuary and I would give you both a lift.

Mrs. Floyd. I have an idea—

Doctor Sam. Oh, have you Connie, whereabouts? Really now? Do you suffer from it—my healthy little wife—show me your tongue.

Mrs. Floyd. Taisez vous—to speak more correctly, I had an idea, and acted upon it, but as I did not wish to lose the benefit of it by discounting a success, I forebore to tell any of you of my plan.

Doctor Sam. Whatever is going to happen when Connie has such a long idea as that?

Mrs. Floyd. Please, Doctor Floyd, I have the floor. We are going to have a visitor this afternoon, dear old uncle Bobbin from Cincinnati. You know he is as rich as a Peruvian gold mine. I wrote to him two weeks ago, telling him all about you four people who want to go housekeeping and have a nice little income to keep it with, and begged him to buy some pictures by Raphael, and a statue by our sculptor brother. I got a letter from him as soon as the return mail could fetch it to me, and he said he had to come to New York on business, and he would visit me, and to make a long story short, I got a telegram this morning that he would be here to-day. I feel it in my bones that he will do something for you.

Gamboge. Dear Mrs. Floyd, your words put fresh hope in our hearts.

Maud. Oh, Connie, you're a dear thoughtful girl.

Connie. Why you said yesterday that I had not but one idea in the world and that was that I had the best husband in America.

Doctor Floyd. You're a sensible little woman and you deserve him, ahem !

Alfresco. I say you are a dear, dear, kind, little sister too.

Connie. Why, you told me yesterday that I was an exasperating little donkey, and the only person I ever tried to please and propitiate was my husband.

Doctor Floyd. Again I say you are a sensible little woman, and if the world were fuller of such it would be the julliest place to live in.

Alfresco. Won't it be splendid if uncle Bobbin does help us. How funny I never thought of writing for his advice.

Maud. If he don't help us, what shall we do to get married ?

Gamboge. Getting married is the easiest part. What shall we live on afterward is the agonizing problem. [*Noise is heard at the door.*]

Mrs. Floyd. I wonder if that is not uncle Bobbin now ? [*Goes to the door.*]

Enter STUMPS *with letter.*

Stumps. A letter for Mr. Gamboge.

Gamboge. Ah, my lad, and why did you not leave it at my studio, is it important?

Stumps. The man that left it said you must get it to wunst.

Gamboge. Any answer?

Stumps. No, sir.

Gamboge. You may go. [*Opens letter.*] Why, what is this? Great heaven! Can he have committed suicide?

Alfresco. What is the matter, dear? No bad news, I hope.

Gamboge. It's from your father. [*Reads*] *By the time this reaches your hand I shall be far away. Macrame lace and raveled rugs fail to compensate me for the loss I have sustained in leaving the art critic's chair on the Fog Whistle. When you made me promise to leave art and go into trade you little knew you had bereft me of the melody of my life. Lest temptation prove too strong, I leave America forever. I shall never be taken alive, so follow me not. With my bride I go to Italy's sunny clime, where beneath its cerulean blue I shall try to forget the ingratitude of the American artists in the study of maiolica. I go; farewell. Barouche Brown.*

Maud and Alfresco. To whom is he married? Oh, papa! to leave us thus!

Connie [*in distress*]. Oh, can it be true? Don't cry, sisters; you shall have a home with us.

Alfresco [*wiping her eyes*]. Who is his bride? Do we know her?

Gamboge. It says in this notice, which he has enclosed, a Miss Cosette Crest.

Alfresco. Cosette!

Maud. Cosette!

Mrs. Floyd. Cosette Crest! It used to be Cosette Crust.

Doctor Floyd. Who the deuce *is* Cosette, anyhow?

Mrs. Floyd. Why, Cosette's our maid.

Doctor Floyd. No, she is not. She is your mother.

Mrs. Floyd. Our mother! I'd like to see myself—

Doctor Floyd. No; but seriously, who is she? or who was she?

Alfresco. She was our maid. Have you forgotten her?

Doctor Floyd. No, for I never remembered her. I never laid eyes on her.

Mrs. Floyd. Oh, what a story! You saw her a hundred times!

Doctor Floyd. Upon my word, I did not.

Gamboge. Neither did I.

Moddle. No more did I.

Gamboge. I don't believe any of us ever saw her, though I confess to having seen on several occasions a pair of ankles; but I never saw the face of the owner; and unobserved, one day, when the noise in the culinary department was the loudest, I took the liberty of making a sketch of them. Here it is.

[*Exhibits sketch of a dreadful pair of ankles. All crowd about it and laugh.*]

Gamboge [*aside to* MODDLE]. What do you think of the news?

Moddle [*aside to* GAMBOGE]. I thought his conversion was mighty sudden. What is the best thing to say to comfort the girls ?

Gamboge. We must marry them at once.

Alfresco [*very proudly*]. Doctor Floyd, you have been a kind, good brother to us, but do not think that we are going to remain a burden on you—Maud and myself are willing to work, and we will go out as governesses, or tend a shop, if we can't do any better. Won't we Maud ?

> [*Puts her arm about her sister and begins to cry.*]
>
> *Enter* BOBBIN *unobserved.*

Gamboge. Dearest Allie, don't cry. [*Goes to her.*]

Moddle. Maud, don't cry, we'll take care of you.

> [*Goes to* MAUD.]

Gamboge. Yes, we have made up our minds, as we cannot live by Art respectably, we will make the fair creature a profound bow, and only remember her as a coy acquaintance. I can get Moddle a position in a clothing store as salesman, and as for me, I'll work for a photographer.

Bobbin [*coming forward*]. Hold your horses. How do you all do ? I know you're all glad to see Uncle Bob, or if you ain't, I'll make you glad before I go. [*Mrs. Floyd rushes into his arms.*] How d'y do? So little Connie's married. How do you like it?

Mrs. Floyd. Oh, Uncle, I'm so glad you have come ! We are in such trouble ! Papa has eloped, and Allie and Maud want to get married, and—

Bobbin. Now don't say another word, I've been listening and heard it all. Young man [*to* GAMBOGE], I like your grit. You keep to them sentiments I heard you say just now, and I'll stand by you. I hear you can paint.

Gamboge. I can paint, but I can't make money.

Bobbin. That's the difference between you and me, I can make money but I can't paint. The only brush I ever handled was when I whitewashed Aunt Betsy's garden fence. And I like your grit, young man. [*To* MODDLE.] So you can make statues.

Moddle. I can make statues, but *I* can't make money.

Bobbin. There's the difference between you and me. I can make money but I can't make statues. Now suppose you listen to an old man who has roughed it and knows the world, if any man does. You two young men marry your girls and come out West with me. I'll give you work if you won't be too high flown to take it. You say you can draw pictures?

Gamboge. By the cartload.

Bobbin. I'll take every one of 'em. You draw 'em and I'll turn 'em all into labels for my soap. For instance a beautiful home, father, mother, children, baby in the cradle.—"The Happy Family," they use Bobbin's soap. Then a sad scene, a man beating his wife—the miserable family, they don't use Bobbin's soap. What's the reason you can't do that? Then you can paint shirts in the laundry where they use Bobbin's Soap, and the shirts in the laundry where they don't use Bobbin's soap. I'll have a man write poetry for each picture. For instance:

Unlaundried shirts long time he wore,
    Sal-soda was in vain,
Till Bobbin's soap came to the fore,
    And set him up again.

Oh, I'm brimful of ideas! It's always been my aim to see pictures of my soap in every grocery store from here to Russia. I can keep you drawing labels for me till you make enough to retire on. Every picture you paint I'll bargain to make it advertise my soap. Say it's a landscape with a girl sitting under a tree or on the door step.

    'Twas a Monday morning,
      Kate's washing was most done,
    And she before the laundry door
      Was sitting in the sun,
    While bleaching on the pretty green,
    Were the whitest shirts you ever seen.

        Chorus. Use Bobbin's soap.

Bobbin's patent quick action, self-asserting, soil-persuading eclectic soap. No respectable family can do without it. It breeds content in the home, comforts the weary housekeeper, lightens the kitchen-maid's cares. The father coming home tired at night to the bosom of his family, sees the effect of Bobbin's soap in the snowy table cloth, the spotless napkins, the children's pinafores, the bath room towels and in the mother-in-law's lace cap. Cleanliness is the first law of nature. It is the foundation of

morals in the family, and the family found the state.   Give Bobbin's soap a trial.   It contains no deleterious substance.   It is perfectly uninjurious to the clothes.

> Give it a trial and ask for more,
> No charge for sample left at your door.

Mrs. Floyd. I say so too, make money and be artistic afterward.

Doctor Floyd. It's my opinion that it's a splendid offer.

Gamboge. And I am thankful for it. I suppose I may have a
chance to paint other pictures in time.

Bobbin. Of course. You needn't take the world into your con-
fidence. You needn't put your name to your pictures of my soap.
I don't care; I ain't proud myself; soap has stuck by me and I'll
stick by soap, but I shall not quarrel with you and the girls if you
don't want to identify A. I. art with the best soap in the United
States. You have your studio in the best building in the city for
your fancy paintings you can't sell, and I'll rig you up a room in
my factory where you can paint the labels you'll make your fortune
at. What's the reason you can't clap a high price on your fancy
pictures, and fight shy of selling them, and then you'll find you
can't paint 'em fast enough for customers; that's human nature.

Moddle. And how can I be of service to you? I don't see how
you can make use of me.

Bobbin. What's the reason I can't give you work? I want you
to make figures of people using Bobbin's soap. I want you to
make a figure of a woman holding a cake of Bobbin's soap in her

hand, with a crown on her head. Why can't art and business mix? If you want to give it an ancient Greek touch, why throw in a little Latin—

> *Semper idem, non disputandem*
> *Soapus Bobbinus ad capitandem.*

Carve it around the bottom of her petticoats, and I'll fix that statue on the highest peak of the Rocky Mountains, if I have to go to Washington twice a year to pay the rent. Don't you fret! I can give you lots of ideas for figures to carry the good news of Bobbin's soap to every grocer in the world—

> From Canada's cold climate
> To old Kentucky's shore
> We'll send a cake of Bobbin's soap
> To every cottage door.

And so forth, and so forth. Now, I'm a man of few words, as perhaps you see. Now, will you take my offer or not?

Gamboge. I'll take it and thank you.

Moddle. And so will I, with all my heart.

Alfresco. Won't it be delightful! and I can paste the labels.

Maud. And I can pose for laundry maids and housewives and Bobbin's soap, the queen of the kitchen.

Bobbin. That's right, I am glad to see you've a straight idea of your duties to your husbands and my soap. Can you get married and ready to go West with me in three days.

All. Oh, yes, yes, yes.

Bobbin. Then I must leave you for a while, for I have other business than making matches. Good-bye until to-night. Bless you my children, and pack your trunks.   [*Exit* BOBBIN.

Gamboge. Now for a fresh start in life; who knows but out there in a new field, free from care, with art boiling the pot and paying the rent, we shall be a hundred times happier than drag-ging out a miserable life of disappointment here—what say you Moddle?

Moddle. I say, "ay" with my whole heart. [*Aside*] *Its rum ain't it?*

Gamboge. It's nothing else, but I'm game for anything. I'll paint the labels at night and peddle the soap in the day time, if the old man insists on it [*aside*].

Moddle. And I'll carry the figures of Bobbin's soap patrons on a board on my head, like an Italian image vender, if I can make a living no other way [*aside*].

Alfresco. We must hurry away and pack our trunks and boxes to emigrate to the far West.

Maud. We must send Benvenuto to that horrid barn to get some things we shall need—where can he be, I sent him of an errand two hours ago.

Gamboge. Whisper of angels and you'll hear their wings.

Enter BENVENUTO.

Ben [*trembling and frightened*]. Oh, Mars Moddle, oh, Miss Frisco, honey.

All. What is the matter, what ails you?

Ben. Dreful news, Miss Frisco.

Gamboge. Tell us quick what is the matter?

Ben. Oh, Mars Gamboge de barn bu'ful's dun sploded. Dar was dynamite in the las' picture dat was sent Mars Brown, an' it done blowed de whole cabin up.

Gamboge. What picture?

Ben. De lilly one wid de curly headed bats.

Gamboge. Curly headed bats!

Ben. Yes, sah!

Alfresco. Why, what can he mean?

Maud. I don't remember it!

Mrs. Floyd [*laughing*]. Perhaps he means the Sistine Cherubs.

Gamboge. Oh, to be sure, the copy by Vert Green. [*Aside* to MODDLE.] You know Brown played the mischief with him in the papers.

Moddle [*aside*]. Yes, I know, but this is a dreadful revenge to take.

Gamboge. Any loss of life, Ben?

Ben. I don' understan you.

Gamboge. Did any one get killed?

Ben. Yes, sah, two ob' em.

Gamboge. Great Heaven! speak quick—not your master and his wife?

Ben. Not zackly, sah—Tabby she los' one ob her eyes, and Towser he had his tail cut smove off.

Gamboge. Oh what a relief. Poor cats! But it might have been worse. And it is quite burned to the ground?

Ben. Yes, sah, clean gone.

Dr. Floyd. And no insurance. [*Laughing.*]

Gamboge. Why then I suppose that is ye last of " Ye *Barn Beautiful.*"

CURTAIN.